Elizabeth Taylor's

NIBBLES
and
ME

Twinkle &
Nibbles playing
together

Elizabeth Taylor's

NIBBLES
and
ME

WRITTEN AND ILLUSTRATED BY

Elizabeth Taylor

SIMON & SCHUSTER BOOKS FOR YOUNG READERS
New York   London   Toronto   Sydney   Singapore

SIMON & SCHUSTER BOOKS FOR YOUNG READERS
An imprint of Simon & Schuster Children's Publishing Division
1230 Avenue of the Americas, New York, New York 10020

Book design by Anne Scatto/PIXEL PRESS
The text for this book is set in Horley Old Style MT.
Printed in the United States of America
2   4   6   8   10   9   7   5   3   1

Library of Congress Cataloging-in-Publication Data
Taylor, Elizabeth, 1932-
Elizabeth Taylor's Nibbles and me / written and illustrated by Elizabeth Taylor.
p. cm.
Originally published: Nibbles and me. New York : Duell, Sloan, and Pearce, 1946.
ISBN 0-689-85334-3
1. Taylor, Elizabeth, 1932- —Juvenile literature. 2. Chipmunks as pets—
Juvenile literature. I. Title: Nibbles and me. II. Title.
PN2287.T18 A3 2002
636.936'4—dc21
2002066985

Dedicated to
Mummie, Daddy, and Howard,
who love Nibbles almost as
much as I do.

Elizabeth and Lassie sign fan mail.

CONTENTS

Nibbles feels perfectly happy sitting on Elizabeth's head.

A NOTE TO THE NEW EDITION

Not so very long ago, somebody asked to see the drawings in *Nibbles and Me*, and I had to rummage around in my library to find a copy, as the book was published more than fifty years ago! This same "somebody" sat down with my book, said she was charmed with my little story, and wondered whether I would consider reprinting it. Well, I thought about it and decided that it couldn't do anybody any harm—after all, no animals are mistreated and no one is especially wicked or even a little awful. What it has are the growing-up observations of a thirteen-year-old girl, perhaps leaving childhood behind, but never, never forsaking her love of animals and the countryside. My hope for any of you young readers is that my little story, and the drawings I made, will make you smile and believe in the magic that a friendship with animals can bring, no matter how old you are. Over the years, animals have remained my sweetest and most cherished friends.

—Elizabeth Taylor
October 2002

PUBLISHER'S NOTE

Nibbles and Me came to us written in a school copybook in the pencilled handwriting of a thirteen-year-old girl. The young girl is Elizabeth Taylor, a charming and unusual actress, who has already been starred in a number of moving pictures. She played Velvet in *National Velvet* and at the time of this book she was acting in *Blue Sierra*.* Elizabeth started to write about the life of her chipmunk, Nibbles, simply out of affection for him—as she wrote, a book developed, and here it is.

* NOTE: *Blue Sierra* was
released as *Courage of Lassie.*

A Note To The Editor —

Dear Mr Editor —

When I wrote this my Daddy was going to have his Secretary copy it out on the typewriter — but the lady at the Studio said she didn't want us to have it typed because she thought you would rather have it as it is —

I do hope you will be able to read it all right. The next day when I would read what I had written the night before, I found it pretty hard to read myself — and such a lot of mistakes I had to errase and correct which makes it rather messy — I start out writing somewhat like I've been taught in school, then the words start tumbling out so fast I can't keep up with them and my writing goes all higgelty piggelty!

I hope it isn't too long It wanted to be longer – but I just had to be firm, and say "No" – after "The Climax" is going to come "The End"

If you have any trouble making it out, I'll be very glad to interpet it for you – If you'd like more drawings I can always do lots more –

Thanking you I remain
Yours Very Sincerely,
Elizabeth Taylor

Elizabeth and Nibbles spend time together.

CHAPTER I

BEFORE NIBBLES

E VER SINCE I was a little girl I have had all sorts of pets. I remember in England at our house in the country there was a nest under the eaves, just outside my bedroom window, with a darling little family of swallows in it. That was why we named our house Little Swallows. It was so beautiful, like a little house out of a Walt Disney film nestled against a lovely woods that was almost like a bird sanctuary. All year around the woods back of our house were carpeted with some kind of wild-flowers, except for just a few weeks during the winter.

I used to ride through the woods on my little mare Betty and I felt so high up in the air among the trees. It seemed as if I was right up there with the birds. They would fly down so low all around me and sing and chatter away—just as if they were trying to attract my attention and talk to me. I used to try and answer them, and sometimes Betty would whinny as if she wanted to talk to us too. She was so intelligent—she knew everything I said to her. Some people say horses do not understand what you say to them—that they only understand the tone of your voice in command—but that *isn't so*. I was only three and a half years old when I first had Betty, and she was as wild as anything, and threw me sky-high into a patch of stinging nettles the first time I crawled onto her back. Then I led her around and talked to her; I told her she had been given to me, and that I was her new mistress, and that I loved her very much and wanted her to love me. We walked around and talked for quite a while, and then I led her over to the stone wall where I could climb up and get on her back, and I kept on talking to her. From then on we were always friends. She would buck other people off or dash into the lake until she frightened them, so that they were glad to get off . . . but you could do anything with her by talking to her. They said I was the only one who could do anything with her, but I know anyone could have if they had loved her as much as I did.

It was such fun down there. You see we lived in

London on Wildwood Road, and we went down to Little Swallows for the summer and weekends. It was so wonderful. I feel I could write a book about Little Swallows. The house was sixteenth century. It was mentioned in Jeffery Farnol's novel, *The Broad Highway*—only then it was supposed to be a haunted house. In fact when we went to live there, lots of people still called it The Haunted House, and it hadn't been lived in for years and years. But we loved it because it looked just as if it belonged in another world.

It had never had a bathroom. So we made the dairy into a bathroom and had to pipe water for fifty miles. One day a messenger boy brought a telegram to the door. I asked him to come in while I called Daddy, and he said, "Come in! Oh no, Miss—not me. This here house is haunted."

Mummie heard him and laughed and said, "Oh, it isn't haunted anymore, now that we've had hot and cold water laid on."

So the rumor soon spread that the Taylors had uprooted the haunts.

We had people actually coming to see the place and raving about how pretty we had made it. There was a fireplace in every room. It was like going to bed in fairyland with the windows all wide open and the firelight flickering on the ceilings and walls, and outside even at night the birds would still sing.

The days were so busy and so exciting with all our pets. My brother Howard (who is two years and eight months older than I am) always had a lot of pets too.

We had rabbits, turtles, snakes, baby lambs, guinea pigs (we started out with two GP's and very soon had fifteen). They were so tiny when they were babies and were so cute to carry around in our pockets. Then we always had kittens all over the place and dogs of all kinds.

But—we never had a chipmunk!

Now if you have never had a chipmunk, you won't know what you have missed. That is why I am writing this, because I think a chipmunk is the nicest *little* pet and companion anyone could possibly have. I say a chipmunk, because I have had a lot of them. I caught twenty-five when we were on location and they were all different. Some were shy and timid, some more daring and bold. One little fellow was so fresh and saucy that I called him Cheeky. (There'll be more about him later.) But the point of it is they were *all little individuals,* and then! there was—

NIBBLES

CHAPTER II

INTRODUCTION TO NIBBLES

To INTRODUCE you properly to Nibbles, I'll have to tell you first of all *how* and *where* he came into my life. It was a year ago this August when we went to Washington on location for *Blue Sierra*. When I read the manuscript, I could hardly wait to get started. The first part of the picture is like a wonderful symphony acted out by all sorts of animals—bears, coyotes, skunks, a fox, a lizard, a squirrel, a beaver, a bobcat, a golden eagle, and a wonderful raven who goes all through the picture. It was going to be such fun with all those animals. And when I heard we were going to Lake Chelan, Washington, to be gone for three months—three months outdoors, every day on the lake and in the woods—it just seemed too good to be true.

Mummie was afraid I would be lonesome without any other children to play with. Sometimes children in pictures have another child for a stand-in. A stand-in is the one who takes your place while the lights and camera are being focused—so you don't get too tired. But I have always had an overage stand-in. That makes it easier for the studio because they can work longer hours. *Overage* sounds pretty old, but it just means over school age. Thelma, my stand-in for *National Velvet,* was just darling. She taught me how to lift a person's head out of their neck. You know, you massage the back of their head and neck, and then give it a gentle pull—that really feels wonderful. I practiced on Mummie and she loves it.

Well, to get back to my story, Mummie was afraid I would be lonesome, but I just could hardly wait. Three months with nothing to do but play with animals.

I was supposed to be a girl living in the apple country on Lake Chelan, who finds a little collie pup that grows up in the end to be Lassie (of *Lassie Come Home*)—only this time he is called Bill. Lassie always was a *he,* you know. His real name is Pal. There were a lot of puppies of different ages to play Bill growing up, and they were all so cute and so easy to train—and here was I going away with them for three months.

It was late in August when we left. It took us three days and two nights to get there. The end of our journey from the village of Chelan up the lake to Moore's Inn (a resort which the studio had taken over for our company) was by boat at night. And what a boat ride that turned out to be! Halfway up a storm came up, and if it hadn't been for the forest ranger's wife (at Land's End, twenty-five miles from Chelan) standing out on the rocks and signaling us to come to her dock, it would have been the watery end perhaps for all of us. One boat of our party which was carrying provisions, and had steamed out just ahead of us, was dashed against the rocks and was sunk. And while the forest ranger was rescuing them, his wife took an enormous flashlight and signaled so frantically to us that we turned in. There were whispered conversations with the skipper and with Mr. Kaplan, our unit manager, and Mummie and I were very curious. We knew something had happened and I knew they were trying to keep it from us. Anyway we were sent back to Chelan by a car to spend the rest of the night, and we didn't know until next morning about the boat being sunk and all hands rescued.

It was lovely the next day and we arrived at Moore's Inn about one o'clock. The first thing I did was to find the animal man, Curley Twyford, who had gone up ahead of us with all the animals, and I guess from then on I was his shadow. He has a way with him that makes you want to learn all that he knows. He can take a wild bird and in a few hours have it eating out of his mouth and doing tricks. I think the nicest compliment I ever had was when he said to Mummie, "That Elizabeth's a great girl. She's got the Twyford touch."

He is the one who gave me my first chipmunk. I'll never forget how thrilled I was when he put that soft furry little thing in my hand. He told me it might bite, but not to worry—it would quit biting if I didn't let it worry or frighten me. I had a string around its neck and I carried it around in my pocket all day. It seemed very shy at first. Then it suddenly ran out of my pocket onto my shoulder and sat there looking straight into my eyes and chirped, and ran around the back of my neck under my hair to the other shoulder and inspected me from that angle. Then it ran up and down all over me and finally came back to nestle under my hair on the

Elizabeth feeds Nibbles.

back of my neck. That was always its favorite place. It was so cuddly and sweet, and after that it never bit me anymore.

When I am making a picture I am always in bed at eight o'clock, and I study my lines from eight to eight-thirty. But up there I seemed to learn them the first time I read them, and so before I went to sleep, Mummie and I would turn the little chipmunk loose in the room and play with him. One of the boys of the crew had made a wonderful big cage—wire all around—and my chipmunk loved it. It had a log in it and turf on the bottom and branches to jump around on, with berries, nuts, seeds, apples, grapes, and brown bread to eat.

Tommie, our wardrobe girl, gave me some cotton wool for a bed for him, and we had more fun tearing it into little pieces and hiding it behind our ears and around places, and he would crawl all over us looking for it. When he found it he would stuff it into his pouches and off he would go to one corner of his box where he was making a nest.

Once when I was playing with him I was called to do a scene and Tommie said, "I'll hold him for you."

I gave him to her and tied the string around his neck like a long leash and onto her finger at the other end.

While I was doing the scene he settled down very nicely on Tommie's knee. She was busy knitting and thought how nice and quiet he was being with her. She hardly breathed to keep from disturbing him. When I came back to get him I picked him up to kiss him and there were his pouches stuffed with bits of Tommie's yellow slacks— and a hole the size of a dollar right over Tommie's knee. He had done it so neatly she didn't even feel it.

Oh, he was so cuddly and sweet! I can hardly write about him without feeling such a pull at my heart, and yet I know that even though he seemed to die, he really just passed from out of my sight; because "Life" doesn't die—it goes on being life whether we see the person or thing it is manifested through or not. When a rose dies—it may look to us withered and brown and dead— but the idea, God's idea, of a rose, that is back of it, doesn't die or there would never be any more roses. The idea is alive—it is life manifested. Bodies are just like roses, when they are gone the idea of life is still just the same. I learned that when my godfather was killed in an airplane crash. Then when Nibbles the first was killed—on the back of my hand as I was bringing his box downstairs to show the animal man his nest, and someone opened the door and caught him between the door and the box—my heart was broken. Mummie and I went up into the woods and cried it out. We walked and walked—and talked about life. And then I knew just as I knew before, that in reality there is no death.

We came back and buried the body of Nibbles the first under a rosebush in the garden back of Moore's Inn, and marked it with a wooden cross we made. And I knew he would always live in my heart—and that another one would come to me . . . not to take his place, but to bring the same sense of love to me, and he did—and I knew him immediately; and I named him Nibbles . . . not Nibbles the second, but just Nibbles—my favorite chipmunk.

CHAPTER III

NIBBLES AS HE WAS— AND IS

N IBBLES CAME from the far end of Lake Chelan, up
past Stehegan, the last post office on the Lake. It was
Daisy Weaver's place—w;..re we took some of the scenes
with the sheep, and where Frank Morgan, who played Old
Harry, was supposed to live. When Mr. Morgan and the
sheep were acting, I was out catching chipmunks. Mrs.
Weaver was very pleased because she said they ate her
garden as fast as it came up. Poor little things, there were
so many of them and they were only looking out for them-
selves—just the way human beings do. Anyway, I was
glad she wanted me to catch them. And when she said that
after the first frost came, the ground would be covered
with their little bodies frozen stiff, I liked catching them
for that reason too, because I was really saving their lives.

I was very careful. When I trapped them in my box and they seemed frightened or unhappy, I let them go. I let several of them out because other chipmunks came up and talked to them and seemed so worried and upset that I was afraid they might be the mother or the father of a family.

They are so little it's hard to tell whether they are male or female. Even the animal man couldn't tell. They all look alike, unless the ones I caught are all the same. Even now, after over a year, no one knows what Nibbles is. But I call him "he" because he is so venturesome and curious and can get himself into such scrapes and

adventures that he should be a "he." I wanted to get a mate for him and raise some babies, but he is so jealous of all the others. After the experience with Cheeky Beggar, which you'll hear more about later, I gave up hope. I decided to let Nibbles live alone and not worry him anymore as he seemed to prefer being a bachelor.

No one knows how old he is—to me he is just like Peter Pan, he will never grow up and never grow old.

When I first caught Nibbles I already had seven others. But I knew he was the one. He knew it too. He was so proud and loved to fluff his tail out and swish it around in grand flourishes, and he would look me straight in the eye and chirp away. He seemed a little disappointed that I didn't chirp back. I tried to but it wasn't quite chipmunk. It was more birdlike—much too high. But he knows what I say to him.

I have him loose in the room now while I write, and he is having the grandest time. He is here one minute and there the next. I have sunflower seeds and pine nuts hidden around the room and when he finds them he runs back to me and hides them in my pocket or a fold of my dress. Oh, just now he climbed up my pencil, then jumped onto my neck and reached up and kissed me, then dashed off down to my big toe where he is balancing himself while eating a seed. Now he is in the wastebasket—he was, I mean—here he is again on my writing paper—in the hollow of my pencil hand.

Oh, he is so cute! He's gone again but not before he kissed me. He stands on my neck with his front feet on my chin and stretches himself so that he can reach my mouth. No matter what he is doing, every few minutes he runs back to kiss me and when he eventually gets tired he'll come back to rest in my pocket or up my sleeve. He is happy with me. I know he is. He keeps showing me that he is—and can you wonder that I love him so much?

Balancing himself on my big toe.

CHAPTER IV

HOW NIBBLES CAME TO HAVE HIS FIRST BUBBLE BATH

NOW TO get back to his adventures.

One day Mummie had a very bad cold—almost pneumonia—and the company doctor wouldn't let her go on location with me. I knew it was best for her not to go, but I knew I would feel lost without her, because when I am doing a picture she is with me all the time. I was afraid she might be lonesome, too, all alone, so I left Nibbles with her. There were seven other chipmunks in their big cage and they were so cute to watch that I thought they would be good company for her. But after I was gone they got to fighting and making such a row that when the doctor came to see Mummie he had the cage moved out into the hall.

Well, somehow, in moving the cage, the trapdoor came

ajar, and out of a sound sleep Mummie was wakened by the wildest chirping and scampering and ping-pinging of wires. She got out of bed and opened the door into the hall and there they were, all eight of them, leaping and jumping about on a pile of bedsprings stacked at the end of the hall just outside our door. It was very cold and Mummie had a high fever and she didn't know what to do. She knew Nibbles was among them but they were all moving so fast that she couldn't tell him from the others, so she decided the only thing to do was to catch them all.

But how? She was so ill, she could hardly stand, so she got a blanket, and wrapped herself up in it, and sat down on the floor in the middle of the hall to keep them from going any farther. She had left the bedroom door open and made a trail of seeds and nuts leading from the springs to inside our room, and there she sat for an hour or more, only moving when one would start to pass her.

Finally she got them all into our room. Then the excitement began. We had twelve suitcases under our beds and stacked in the clothes closet that only had a curtain on it instead of a door.

Poor Mummie! If you've ever tried to catch a chipmunk like that, you know how fast they can run.

They climbed the curtains. They jumped from the top

of one curtain rod to another. They were running up and down our clothes . . . in and out among the suitcases . . . Mummie said it was like a madhouse. She caught one of them and he bit her so hard, she let him go. Then she went into the bathroom and through Mrs. Barringer's (my schoolteacher's) room into the hall and brought the cage back that way into our room. She put it on the floor with both of its doors open, hoping they would go in. Then she went back into the bathroom and peeked around the corner to see what they would do. After a while, when all was very quiet except for their chirping, some of them went in and out of the cage.

Then while she was standing there—Nibbles—the adventurous one, decided to explore the bathroom. He ran across her toes up her dressing gown; Mummie hardly dared to breathe hoping he would come up high enough to let her catch him, because even when she started to move her hand he was so frightened . . . but no . . . he was off in a flash . . . and with a loud splash he landed plunk in the middle of the toilet bowl.

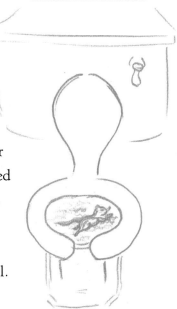

His First Bubble Bath

It was clean water, but even so, he was panicky. The sides of the bowl were shaped so he couldn't get out and he would have drowned if Mummie hadn't reached in and fished him out.

Poor Nibbles—wet and shivering—with all of his bravado well wetted down. There was only one thing to do—give him a bath, with a dash of ST 37 in it. Mummie held him in one hand and soaped him with the other. Then, to sweeten him up, she gave him some of my pine-oil bubble suds.

So that was how Nibbles came to have his first bubble bath.

Mummie dried him and put him in her pocket to keep him warm until he fully regained his composure. Then he was quite content to go into his traveling dressing room (that I use on location). Mummie put him in there all by himself until his sweet smell wore off, as she was afraid the other chips might turn up their noses at him and think he'd gone Hollywood.

CHAPTER V

INTO A NEST
OF SNAKES

T HE NEXT scrape that Nibbles got himself into was quite an adventure for us, too. It was Sunday afternoon—no school, and nothing to do but play with Lassie and the puppies and, of course, Nibbles.

We were out on the lawn in front of Moore's Inn, all gathered around a big stone fireplace that stood quite alone. It was sort of like a barbecue that hadn't been used for years and was covered with ivy. For some reason or other there was a wire fence about three or four feet high all around the fireplace. It was just near the boat landing. We were all sitting there, waiting for the mail boat to come in. We knew there was a nest of snakes between the wire and the stone work of the fireplace because we had counted six of them that afternoon.

There he was on top of the fireplace.

Elizabeth, Frank Morgan, and Lassie on location

Well, we were all playing and Nibbles had been bur-
rowing in Lassie's lovely long coat, when a big sheep dog
started barking and frightened Nibbles and he made one
dive for the fireplace.

I screamed for everyone to watch out for him. They
all gathered around and we searched everywhere for
him. We all looked for hours, but no sign of him. Then it
came six-thirty and dinnertime. They all went in except
Mummie and me. We couldn't. My heart was breaking.
Mummie tried to comfort me and she said, "Don't you

see, darling, if it's right for him to be your chipmunk, and if it makes him happy, too, he'll come back to us—now that they've all gone inside and we're here alone—and if he doesn't, promise me you won't cry or worry."

I couldn't promise anything and Mummie didn't ask me to anymore. We just sat there staring at the fireplace. We both somehow knew he was still there even though we had felt all around it with sticks and no sign of him . . .

Presently high above the wire fence we heard a movement and a little tiny chirp, and there he was on top of the fireplace looking down at us.

We didn't say a word to each other, but both of us moved up to the wire, pulled it down, and climbed over into the place where the snakes were crawling. Then Mummie held me up where I could reach him, and Nibbles crawled out onto my hand.

He *wanted* to be my chipmunk! Oh, can you imagine how I felt? I cried and cried for joy, and Mummie did too. But I don't mind telling you, with Nibbles safe in my pocket we couldn't get out of that snake's nest fast enough. Mummie was shaking all over, 'cause she hates snakes.

Elizabeth and her brother Howard

CHAPTER VI

I DO
A TRAPEZE
ACT OUT
MY WINDOW

S UNDAY SEEMED to be our big day, or rather
Nibbles's big day, for getting into mischief. He
could think of more things come Sunday. I think he
saved them up all week.

This particular Sunday, Eleanor, the hairdresser
(Eleanor and Tommie, the wardrobe girl, were with us
all through *National Velvet,* and we just love them both),
had washed my hair and was setting it with pin curls. I
was playing with Nibbles when someone outside my window called me, and with Nibbles on the back of my hand,
I went to the window and opened the screen.

There was a vine with little red berries all over the building, and Nibbles, like any other chipmunk, scampered off

to feast on the berries. I couldn't see where he had gone. I was panicky and started out the window head first. Fortunately, Eleanor grabbed one foot and Tommie the other and they held on to me while I dangled head down. Then I saw Nibbles. He was sitting on the vine looking up at me with his big eyes saying "Here I am." I could hardly reach him, but he hopped toward me, onto my arm, and into my hand.

Mummie rounded the corner of the building just as Tommie and Eleanor were hauling me in. They were worn out! I guess I am more or less like a young horse, at least I'm no featherweight to go dangling out windows, but aside from it being a little rough on certain developing places, I was no worse for wear.

On the way in I grabbed a big bunch of berries, and so Nibs was very happy.

I set him free - on the grass.

CHAPTER VII

HIS FIRST AND LAST APPEARANCE IN PICTURES

O NE DAY we were doing a scene on a little wooden platform—a sort of lookout high above Lake Chelan where Kathie (that's the girl I am in the picture) used to sit and look for Bill (that's Lassie). In the story Bill gets lost from her when he is herding the sheep and she is up a tree eating apples. A truck runs over him and the drivers take him to a dog hospital, and then because no one knows whom he belongs to, they enlist him in the army. . . . Kathie looks for him day after day. She goes out in her sailboat one day, calling and looking for him when a terrible storm comes up. It turns the boat over and she almost drowns. It really was a terrible storm, too, and to make it worse someone told us that when anyone went down in the lake they never came up again, they just kept going on down.

Anyway to get back to my story . . . Kathie was on her lookout—gazing out over the water and grieving for Bill. We were sitting around waiting for a cloud to come and make a pretty background. In Technicolor you spend hours waiting for clouds—pretty, white, fluffy ones—and usually by the time they come the sun is gone and you have to stop for the day. I took Nibbles out and he crawled up my arm and sat on my shoulder looking straight at me.

It was the sweetest thing. I think he thought I was really grieving, and I guess I was 'cause I always do when I'm supposed to. Anyway he looked so concerned, and the director (Freddie Wilcox, who directed *Lassie Come Home*) saw him, and called the cameraman (Lenn Smith, who has been my cameraman ever since *Lassie*). They thought it would be wonderful to put Nibbles in the scene—just as he had put himself into it. Then the camera would move in for a big close-up of both of us.

I was so happy to have him in the picture with me, and he was so good. As he didn't have a stand-in, we had to stand in together while the lights and camera were being set. Nibbles sat so still, he didn't bat an eyelash. During the take I couldn't look at him—I had to be looking out over the water—but that was one time I wasn't feeling anything but tickled all over. I was thinking how cute Nibbles looked. They had to do the scene over several times to get me over being tickled and into the mood.

And now I hear that after all that beautiful acting on Nibbles's part, they cut his scene right out. He was *too* good. He didn't look real.

CHAPTER VIII

CONCERNING HIS FIRST TRAIN JOURNEY

S OON AFTER Nibs's first and last appearance, we finished all the location scenes and were ready to come back to the studio. We had been there almost three months and it was getting colder and they didn't want us to get snowed in and have to stay all winter. Already the top of the mountains around were covered with snow, and I felt so unhappy to think of all the little chipmunks that would be frozen. If I could only bring them all home to California!

As soon as I knew when we were leaving I had a lot to do getting my family organized for the journey. One of the crew made a darling little traveling box or dressing room for Nibbles. The others were to come on the animal boat, with all the other animals we had used in the picture.

A day or two before we were to leave I got to worrying about Nibbles being lonely and decided he should have a traveling companion to share his private box. So I turned all the chipmunks loose in the room to see which one Nibbles seemed to like best. I gave them all some seeds and nuts, and Nibbles immediately scampered up the curtain and hid his in some folds at the top. He sat there guarding his treasures. At the approach of any of the others he would jump at them and chase them away. Then Cheeky came bounding up to him.

He chirped at Nibbles, and with a nonchalant flourish of his tail, he dived right into Nibbles's store of treasures and came up with a nice big walnut. He sat calmly beside Nibbles eating it as if all the world belonged to him—and to him quite alone. Nibs was really taken aback at such cheek. But I think he admired it, too, because he didn't say a word or flick a whisker. He just went on eating. They finished their first course and then came scampering down for a bit of chocolate.

That did it. For Nibbles to share chocolate with anyone meant that they met with his approval. So I immediately packed two bags of nuts, two neat packages of wool for bedding, and Cheeky Beggar was elected as his companion.

I cleared my school satchel of books and put Nibbles's box in it. The box had wire on one side, so they could get plenty of air, and Nibbles and Cheeky Beggar seemed quite thrilled and very curious over the prospect of a train journey, and I was thrilled, too, because I thought at last I had found a mate for Nibbles and come spring we would have a family.

All went very well on the boat coming down Lake Chelan. They were so good and quiet no one knew I had them with me. But the first night on the train they were holy terrors. Our drawing room was at the end of an old-fashioned coach and every time the train stopped and all was quiet, they would start screaming and yelling at each other in their *worst* chipmunk language. It was really terrible, and I would swing down from my upper berth and bang on their box and tell them to stop it!

Nibbles would poke his nose out the wire for me to stroke, and I would tell him that I loved him and that he was to be a good boy. But Cheeky was very indifferent and didn't care a hoot whether she was good or not. I say "she" because at that time I was hoping it was a "she." Later we decided she must have been a "he" or they would have gotten along better.

The journey home was without incident except for the wrangling of the chips, which kept up all the way.

Daddy and Howard met us at Glendale and, oh!, we were so glad to see them. Then, when we got home to Beverly Hills and saw all the dogs and cats, it was wonderful. They were all over us. Monty, our English golden retriever, put his paws on my shoulder and his head in the curve of my neck and groaned and cried for joy at seeing us. Twinkle, my little cocker spaniel, couldn't reach that far but she kept jumping up in the air until I caught her in my arms. She is so funny. . . . When we pet the other dogs, she is so jealous and throws herself around banging into them, trying to knock them away. But Spot, the springer spaniel, is the real comedian. She gets so excited, she puts her head down just as if she were trying to stand on her head—by that time Twinkle will have given her a bang and sent her sprawling, and she'll look at you with a laugh on her face just as if that was what she was trying to do in the first place.

They were all very curious about the new addition to our family. If sniffing says anything in dog and cat language, there certainly was a lot of conversation going on about those chipmunks.

By this time Nibbles had a piece of skin taken out of his nose, by—apparently—Mr. Cheeky Beggar, so I had to separate them. Nibbles was very pleased to reign supreme again in his own home, and he tore his bed apart and had a thorough, good housecleaning.

Cheeky, who had convinced us she was no lady, was much happier, too, in a house of "his" own, which Howard quickly stirred up out of an apple box.

The next day I could hardly wait to get to the studio to show all the children and all my friends Nibbles. I put a string around his neck and put him in my pocket. Can you imagine how surprised everyone was? Some of the stars (ladies) screamed and thought he was a mouse . . . but when he swished and fluffed up his tail they thought he was darling. He completely won them over.

The first day I took him to lunch with me in the commissary, he caused quite a furor. I was afraid they would make me take him out, and when Howard Strickling, the head of the publicity department, telephoned to the commissary for me to come to his office, I thought we were in for it. As Mummie and I walked into Mr. Strickling's office, Nibs poked his head out of my pocket and I was all but trembling. Then Mr. Strickling said, "Well, Elizabeth, we've had a discussion about your chipmunk. As you know animals *are not allowed* in the commissary—*but*—in this particular case, I want you to know that we have decided to make an exception. We are *delighted* with the behavior of Nibbles."

Aren't people wonderful?

After that Nibbles went with us everywhere.

When the Christmas holidays came and Nibbles and I went shopping, people begged to know where they could get a chipmunk. I just wished I had all the ones that by that time would be frozen up at Lake Chelan. I wanted so much to start a chipmunkery and raise them so that I could give them to people who loved them.

I did give away most of the ones that came down on the animal boat. I only kept five. They had been in one cage and they were in a dreadful state when they arrived. They had fought so with each other. One poor little thing was almost dead. We called him Little Joe. Mummie saved his life by holding him in her hand and putting some stuff the vet gave her on his leg, which was almost eaten off. One night she held him from eight-thirty until eleven o'clock, and the next morning he could hold himself up. After about a week the skin healed over and he could walk. We had to make separate houses for all of them.

Everyone loves Nibbles. He has even had interviews. The nicest ones were with Maxine Arnold of *Photoplay* and Sara Salzer of *Screen Guide*. And how he loves having his picture taken! From his photographs and interviews he receives lots of fan mail. I'm afraid I have to answer it for him as he is busy all the time making and remaking his bed. He chews it up into bits which he stuffs in his pouches and rearranges it from there. . . . Then too he has to store up things for the winter. It's a little too warm in California to hibernate, but he plays safe by getting prepared anyway. I guess he doesn't want to take any chances with our unusual weather.

CHAPTER IX

CONCERNING CHRISTMAS

NIBBLES WAS so surprised at Christmastime when we brought in a large Christmas tree. He chirped and had a lot of fun running up and down and jumping from branch to branch. But he seemed to be a little disgusted with us when we started trimming the tree with ornaments and hanging tinsel on it. One very ancient Father Christmas that we've had on the tree ever since I was a little girl, he fairly tore to bits and made off with his beard. He liked the gingerbread men and candy sticks. But the minute he eats anything he has to sit up and wash and the peppermint sticks got on his whiskers and stuck to his teeth and made him furious.

I think he thought we were crazy on Christmas morning when we started unwrapping presents with all the accompanying squeals of delight. We have a lot of fun. You see we have the animals all in, except the horses, and have a stocking stuffed full for each one of them . . . catnip and rubber balls and mice for the cats . . . rubber bones, a few sweets, dog biscuits, and new collars for the dogs . . . and they get just as excited as we do.

Nibbles didn't know what to think. Then I started unwrapping his presents and I never realized until then how choosy a chipmunk could be. He had a beautiful green and gold cage given to him with a wonderful wheel in it to exercise on. It was such a gorgeous affair—and I thought he'd be delighted because he is so curious and in this cage he could see on all sides at once. But not a bit of it. He hated it and made no pretense of liking it. He jumped at it with all four feet and spat at it. He even scolded me for *thinking* he would like it . . . and bless his heart how right he was, because it *was* silly to give it to him in the wintertime when he should have been hibernating. (He loves it now for a nice airy cool summer house.) Fortunately Daddy and Howard had made a wonderful winter home for him out of a mahogany night table. It pleased him just as much as the gold cage annoyed him. It is painted to match my room, and just has wire across one side. Inside it has a wonderful log

that Daddy hollowed out partway—where he can store nuts and seeds—which is instinct for them to do whether they have to or not. Then there is a place for water, and for his daily half orange.

He was so cute. He just loved it and right away started making his bed in one corner. I put a little pink wool doll's blanket in for him, and a nice fresh wad of cotton wool, and he made his bed under the blanket. As he added more wool the blanket kept getting higher and higher off the floor until it stood up about three inches. Then he went in to try it out. I lifted up one corner of the blanket to peek at him and there he was in his dear little downy nest with a hole in the middle for his nose to poke out. He stuck his head out to look at me as if to say, "OK." Then he dozed off to dream—I daresay of the strange things he had seen on the Christmas tree.

He didn't rest for long, though, for his next package consisted of pine nuts which he almost went crazy over. And what a time he had hoarding them away in his hollow log.

His next present, I am sorry to say, completely cowed him. It was so thoughtfully worked out and sent to him by a friend of mine in the publicity department. But still he didn't like it. It was a lovely long gold chain for a leash with a dear little gold ring on one end for my finger and a collar for Nibs on the other end with a nameplate on it. When I put it on him, he just sat and stared as if he had been put in the stocks. He was terrified of it. It's the only thing I have ever seen faze him. So I took it off and hung it on the green and gold cage. . . . His two dislikes. At least, I was glad to see that he openly showed his likes and dislikes.

The other chipmunks came in for pine nuts and all sorts of goodies, but Nibbles, being such an established character as he is, was the only one to receive "outside" presents. Thelma, my stand-in, made him some leads and a collar out of crochet thread, which he loved. In fact, he really had a big day—almost as big as I did.

Howard and I together received five saddles. We could hardly wait to get out to the Dufee Stables where we board our horses—Prince Charming, my two-year-old colt that Mr. Pasternak gave me, and Sweetheart, Howard's two-year-old filly—to take them their presents. Nibbles went along. He sat in his old dressing room and watched us ride. I was glad in a way that he didn't like his fancy new gold cage and chain. It showed he had character. Famous or not, he was going to stay *the same*—and I knew how right he was.

When we were doing *National Velvet,* Mr. Brown, the director, was very cross one day because someone put a gold star on my dressing room and "Miss" Taylor on the door. He made them take it away and put ELIZABETH on instead. He was afraid I would be hurt about it, and he explained that he was afraid it might go to my head—or wherever it does go that makes people change—and he wanted me always to stay the same. I knew what he meant because Mummie and I had talked it over before, and I promised him with all my heart that I would *never, never* change. And I won't . . . I couldn't—anymore than Nibbles could.

CHAPTER X

CONCERNING, AMONG OTHER THINGS, MY MOST WONDERFUL BIRTHDAY

THERE IS always somewhat of a letdown after Christmas. It seems such a long time before Christmas can come again. We drag it out as long as possible at our house. Every night, from Christmas Eve until Twelfth Night, when we take the tree down, Mummie plays and we sing carols and we pop corn and sit around the fire. It's such a wonderful holiday. It's always over too soon.

But this year was different! When the tree came down and the ornaments were all packed away, there still was Nibbles. . . . His funny little antics and his loving little ways make every day seem like Christmas and Easter all rolled into one. It's just as if he went straight to your heart and tickled it.

Speaking of tickling reminds me of one day when we were going to an interview and we ran into Hedda Hopper. She was all dressed up and looking very lovely, and I introduced her to Nibbles. She thought he was darling, and put out her hand to him whereupon he, with one grand swish of his beautiful tail, leaped lightly onto her hand. He ran straight up her arm, under her coat sleeve! Now if you've never had a chipmunk run around under your arm, you just can't imagine how it feels. It's the most terrific tickle in the world. I'm used to it, but poor Hedda wasn't. She screamed and laughed a wonderful laugh that made everyone run out just in time to see her skinning out of her coat like a streak of lightning. Everyone was roaring—everyone but Nibbles.

Since then Nibbles has learned a lot about etiquette. He knows now that sleeves are taboo—all except mine.

Nibbles meets everybody. I took him up to call on Ida Koverman and Mr. Louis B. Mayer. He sat on my shoulder looking at Mr. Mayer—just as if he knew who he was, and that he ought to remember his manners. When we were ready to leave he crawled down on the back of my hand, then paused—sat up on his haunches, and gave himself a quick wash and brush up. Then he hopped over onto Mr. Mayer's shoulder and looked up at him as if to say, "Well, good-bye, Mr. Mayer, this has indeed been a great pleasure!" When I took him to *Modern Screen*'s birthday party he met Louella Parsons, Esther Williams, Van Johnson, and Robert Walker. We were all photographed together. Only once did he forget his manners, and then just for a minute when he crawled on top of the cameraman's head and started burying a bit of cake in his hair. He loves cake, and ice cream with hot chocolate sauce.

Our mutual fondness for ice cream was partly the reason for my breaking my foot. We had lingered over our dessert a bit too long when we suddenly realized it was almost time for my singing lesson. I was learning *Summertime*, one of my favorite songs, and I didn't want to be a minute late, so I handed Nibbles to Mummie and said, "Take Nibs and I'll run on ahead."

I had hardly said it before I lunged forward, but my right foot stayed on the floor (my heel caught on a seam of the linoleum) and my body with all the horsepower of my forward lunge came down on my foot. I heard the bone break. I screamed, it hurt so, and I couldn't move. Mummie and a policeman lifted me up and the chief of police called the ambulance. They took me to the hospital.

It's awful on the lot when you hear the ambulance coming, everyone is so worried and wonders who it is and what's happened. It always makes one feel very unhappy, and so when they took me in the ambulance and I saw everyone looking so sad, I sat up and laughed very loud and waved to them, so they wouldn't feel unhappy but would just think I was having a joyride. And they did. They thought that Nibs and I were up to some mischief. When the doctor set my foot and put it in a cast I held on tight to Nibbles's dressing room and I got to thinking how glad I was that I didn't have him in my hand when I fell, and while I was feeling grateful about that, the first thing I knew the cast was on—and we had weathered that storm or another adventure together.

The next big event in our lives was my birthday. To me it was going to be wonderful because I was going into my teens! But little did I know how really wonderful it was going to be until the very day . . . February twenty-seventh.

The one thing in the world I wanted, and which I had always wanted from the day I first saw him, was King Charles (or The Pi, as he was called in *National Velvet*). I had finally talked Mummie and Daddy into letting me buy him, and every day for a week I had been

Elizabeth and Nibbles play with a toy horse.

Elizabeth with Mickey Rooney in *National Velvet*

going up to Mr. Thau's office, but he was off the lot and didn't come in. So the day before my birthday I was feeling so low because I didn't even know whether they would sell him to me or not, now that he was a big star, getting fan mail and all, and him costing such a lot of money. My heart was very heavy and I told Marjory Reeves, Mr. Thau's secretary, all about it. She said, "Don't worry, Elizabeth, you go home and be happy and I'll talk to Mr. Thau about it when he comes in."

Marjory is so sweet and understanding and I knew it was in good hands. So Nibbles and Mummie and I went home.

To make a long story short, the next day—the most wonderful birthday in all my life—Marjory called up and said, "Happy Birthday, Elizabeth, and Mr. Thau wants to speak to you."

My heart stood still, and then as I heard what he had to say I screamed, "Jeepers." Mummie said I screamed "Jeepers" three times, and jumped straight up in the air each time, Nibbles on my shoulder jumping with me, and the tears rolling down my face. Just thinking about it now, and remembering, I still want to scream and jump, and I can still hear Mr. Thau saying, "Elizabeth, we're *giving* you King Charles for your birthday!"

I don't know what else he said—or at that moment there were no other words in the world. King Charles was mine—all mine.

If you've ever loved a horse as I love that horse, you'll understand—and if you haven't there's no use trying to explain.

CHAPTER XI

HOW WE JOURNEY FORTH INTO ONE OF NIBBLES'S SCARIEST ADVENTURES

THE DAYS that followed were divine. I rode King every day. I groomed him, I—but I mustn't go on any more about him, because he could fill a book all by himself, and this is supposed to be about the adventures of Nibbles.

It all started on the third of July—a week after school closed. Daddy and Mummie had arranged with the studio that I was to have a month's holiday out of town, away from all appointments and everything. We were going fishing with Uncle Howard in northern Wisconsin.

My brother Howard, who was named after Uncle Howard, had

gone on ahead of us, all by himself. So it was just Mummie, Daddy, and me. Of course, Mummie knew that I could no more go without Nibbles than she could go without me, but Daddy was quite taken aback when Mummie broke it to him that Nibbles was going too. You see, he had never traveled with a chipmunk before, and somehow felt it wasn't just the thing to do. But Mummie soon made him see that even though it wasn't being done, in this case it was the only thing to do. Anyway, he was too little to leave behind, and that was soon settled. I think I am very lucky to have a mummie and daddy who love pets too. Life would be difficult if they didn't.

Nibbles was terribly excited about another train journey. Our cook had packed a wonderful lunch box of fried chicken, olives, celery, carrot sticks, tomatoes, potato salad, baked ham, cheese, all kinds of fruit, cake and fudge, a thermos of coffee for Mummie and Daddy, and milk for me. And for Nibbles I had packed sunflower seeds, watermelon seeds, little oranges (which he loves), apples, nuts, and raisins. He ate our cake and candy.

The first night on the train I put a string on him and let him exercise, so he would sleep well, but the next day he was having such fun we decided to let him run loose in our room. We locked the doors and he had a wonderful time running, jumping, and exploring. Then all of a sudden he disappeared. I called and called him, but not a sound. Mummie and Daddy kept trying to tell me that he was all right, just resting somewhere, but I knew different. We looked under the beds—we threw seeds around to get him to come out—but no sign of him. My heart sank. I knew something dreadful had happened. Why, oh, *why!*, had we let him out?

Then, a way off, I heard a scratching noise, and the pipes along the floor sounded as if something was tapping them. I put my ear to the floor and listened. I heard it again, and I cried out "Nibbles!" I put my head down close to the pipes and kept talking and calling to him. I could hear him coming nearer and nearer. It was as if he was scratching the pipes to let me know he was coming.

Finally, after what seemed like hours, he came into sight. There he was between the pipes, *back* of the metal mesh work that enclosed them. But how had he gotten there, and how were we going to get him out? He kept trying to get out—back and forth—but there seemed no way. But I knew there would be a way if we could just keep him calm.

Elizabeth plays with Nibbles.

We all sat perfectly quiet and I just hummed a song, one that I'm always singing, so he would hear my voice. He was quiet for a moment and then disappeared—and the next instant he was there in my lap. My hands and my heart closed joyfully around him, and as he snuggled into their warmth I cried for joy that he was home safe.

After that adventure his exercise on the train consisted of running up and down my coat sleeve on the end of a string.

CHAPTER XII

OF OUR ARRIVAL AND WHAT WAS ALMOST A SORRY END

W E ARRIVED at Uncle Howard's house on Lake
Kiwangesagee (or Lake Minocqua, as it is
sometimes called) a few days before Uncle Howard
arrived. Aunt Mabel, Uncle Howard's wife, stayed in
New York this year instead of coming to Wisconsin. She
was under a doctor's care and didn't feel like the long
trip. But she made Uncle Howard come anyway. Ed, the
caretaker, Margaret, the cook, and Rintha, the maid, all
loved Nibbles and we made a nice big house for him to
live in in my bedroom. I was a little worried for fear
Uncle Howard might not approve of a chipmunk in the
house, and I thought if he didn't we'd both have to move
out to the quarters next to the garage. You see, when

There he was looking
looking completely dazed
+ bewildered by it all

people haven't had children of their own they're not used to having chipmunks and things around.

But fortunately for us Uncle Howard loved Nibbles and he thought it was wonderful for me to have such a wonderful little pet and companion. He said as long as I loved chipmunks and horses, I was safe. Oh, I'm getting ahead of my story. Nibs's next hair-raising adventure happened the day or the morning after we arrived, *before* Uncle Howard came.

Mummie and I had slept late, and when she came in to call me, I asked her to help me inspect the room to see if it was safe to let Nibbles out. We closed the ventilator and saw that the screens were fastened, and looked all around to see that there were no other danger spots. Then we turned him loose. When I went in for my bath I called out to Mummie to watch him for me. She stretched out on my bed reading and I could hear her laughing every so often as Nibs would run up and kiss her, then go tearing off—that always tickled so. Then it was very quiet.

I came out to find Mummie sitting up in bed looking very white. She said, "Go get Daddy."

I thought she was ill and ran into Dad's room. When we came back Mummie was pulling my bed out from the wall, and there on the wall back of my bed was an open hot-air ventilator place.

Then I knew what had happened. I ran to it, and called, "Nibbles, Nibbles!"

I was crying by that time, as all I could think of was that he would be roasted alive. The mornings and evenings were cool enough to have the heat on. While I was crying and calling him, Mummie told Daddy to get Ed and go to the basement and see if they could get Nibbles out. She had heard him drop down and land at the bottom of the vent. Then in a flash Mummie had a nail file and was unscrewing the metal front of the vent. She had it off in a minute. We looked down but could see nothing but a big round metal pipe. Not a sign of Nibbles, not even a sound. We kept talking and calling very gently to him. Then we heard Daddy, Ed, and Howard, down in the basement, trying to take the thing apart to get to him. Oh, it was awful! I couldn't budge from the opening. I kept calling him. Mummie quickly tied all our dressing-gown cords and sashes together and we tied it to the bed and dropped it down the opening—and waited—we scarcely breathed for listening—but not a sound from him. I felt I couldn't bear it any longer. Mummie said, "Dress quickly. We'll have to do something."

We both started tearing into our clothes. My head and my heart were bursting with agony. Then I heard Mummie groan, "Oh, *look,*—darling!"

And there in the middle of that black opening sat poor little Nibbles—looking completely dazed and bewildered by it all.

We could have screamed for joy, but he looked so weak and frightened that I just stretched out my hand to him. And it was just as if he heaved a sigh as he crawled into my hand and snuggled down. Can you imagine how I felt? I wanted to go off and cry and cry. I felt shaky all over for hours afterwards.

It was a jolly good thing for Uncle Howard's house that Nibbles appeared just when he did, because in another few minutes we'd have been down in the basement taking the furnace apart. Then I'm afraid he would not have been such a welcome house guest.

Elizabeth and Nibbles in the garden

CHAPTER XIII

I MAKE A HEARTBREAKING DECISION AND NIBBLES MAKES HIS CHOICE

A FTER THAT Howard boarded up the ventilator, but it wasn't really necessary. Nibbles had learned his lesson. He shied quite clear of the thing. In fact for a while it seemed to take the edge off of his curiosity. He was quite content to sit and smell the flowers. Only he wouldn't smell them, he would tear them apart. He loved to sit on the back of a chair looking out the window.

One day he sat there so long and so still, looking out of the window, my heart began aching for him . . . wondering what he was thinking . . . whether he would like to be out in the woods where he really belonged. I sat there watching him . . . with my heart breaking with the thought of what I was trying to make myself do . . . *open the screen and let him go!*

I felt I'd die if I did, but I knew I wouldn't. I felt my heart would break if he went off and I never saw him again. And yet I felt if *he wanted* to go, it was wrong to keep him.

I talked it over with Mummie. I knew she would understand how I felt because she loves Nibbles too. She said, "It's up to you, darling, to make your own decision."

I *couldn't decide!* So I went for a walk in the woods. My heart was crying out for the answer. Then it came.

Howard called to me to come and see a chipmunk he had caught in a trap. I went over to him and there was such a poor, frightened, frantic little animal—panicky at the sight of human beings. Howard said, "Isn't he a beauty?"

But to me he was just pitiful. I said, "Oh, please, Howard, let him go—"

And he said, "Why don't you let Nibbles go if you feel so sorry?"

Then I told Howard that I was trying to let Nibbles go, and I asked him to help me be strong—and not mind about the heartache. He said I should let him go, that we

He would sit balancing on one daisy while he tore
the others apart.

One day he sat there
so long & still,
looking out
the window.

could turn them both loose together. He waited for me on the lawn while I went in to get Nibbles.

The world at that moment seemed so black and empty. I met Mummie in the hall. We didn't say a word, but she seemed to know. She held me close in her arms, and the tears rolled down both our cheeks. Then Daddy called and she had to go. I went into my room. I couldn't stop crying. I knew I would cry for days, but that didn't matter—I must go through with it—quickly. I leaned over and Nibbles hopped onto my arm—and together we hurried out of the house.

Howard said, "I'll bet you won't let him go."

Then I said, "Oh Howard, don't—don't say anything."

I held Nibbles to my face and kissed and kissed him. I couldn't see—my eyes were so blinded with tears—but the feel of his dear little body I'll never forget. I leaned down and set him free on the grass—then Howard opened the trap and let his chipmunk out. Like a streak, he dashed past Nibbles and was off into the woods just a few feet away. Nibbles fluffed out his tail and chirped and started off. I thought that was the end of everything—*but he did look happy*—that was something. He ran to the edge of the wood where the other chipmunk had gone . . . then he stopped to eat an acorn he found. My heart cried out to him, "Good-bye, Nibbles"—and then—the next thing I knew—he ran to me and jumped up on my skirt and *into my hand,* where he gaily perched and finished his acorn.

Oh, I can't describe what I felt! Mummie came running out of the house. She had been watching from a window . . . *Then* there was no more doubt. He was *mine—by his own choice!* And he was as happy as I was—as we all were.

Then he stopped — to eat an acorn.

CHAPTER XIV

V-J DAY IN CHICAGO

AFTER THAT it was such a happy holiday. We fished and had wonderful picnics. We went for long walks through the woods—and I learned some new birdcalls. I would listen to them and then copy them and it got so they would answer me back—and would fly along through the trees calling to me. They would come right up to the clearing where the lawn began. Then they would fly away.

All too soon came the time to go home. Howard stayed on to finish out the summer. We left Wisconsin in the morning, and the news of V-J Day came just as we were pulling out of Milwaukee.

A soldier and his bride got on the train in a shower of

rice. The whistles were all blowing. People were leaning out of windows screaming and yelling. The soldier with his bride looked so happy. I kept watching her face—*it* didn't look anything. I wanted her to look at him, but she kept looking out of the window. It worried me. Was she putting on an act or what? Here was all the world so happy, and here was she, a bride, and she looked so bored. Why should she have been a bride and not be happy about it? Maybe some folks think that is the proper way to act—not to show your feelings in public. But I know when I'm a bride I'll be grinning all over my eyes and nose and mouth.

Nibbles felt the excitement in the air, and I guess he must have felt my interest in the bride and groom, too, because he became very curious and crawled up the back of the bride's chair, and nibbled on some rice that fell out of her hair. Then I put him on the floor (on the end of a string) and he ate up all the rice—and, at last, he got even the bride to smile. After that we all felt better.

When we arrived in Chicago the town was wild. A nice man from the MGM office met us with a car and took us to our hotel where we were to stay until the next night. He wanted to take us out in the car that night to

Elizabeth and Nibbles have breakfast together.

see the crowds, but we wanted to walk and *be* part of the crowd—not just looking at it.

So after dinner we left the hotel and walked down Michigan Boulevard. I'll never forget that night—nor the next day, of which you'll hear more in a minute. We were so surprised to find in all the excitement that crowds of people recognized me as "Velvet" and wanted my autograph. It made me feel very happy. I felt dazed by all the noise.

We kept saying to each other, "Just think, it's over!"

And I kept thinking . . . now Howard won't ever have to go, and I knew Mummie and Daddy were thinking the same thing. But it was sad thinking of the ones who would never come back.

We went into a beautiful church, and sat there almost alone, and prayed. Why didn't more people come in to pray and thank God? There were only a dozen or so when we were there. . . . But I'm sure they were praying in their own way wherever they were.

We walked until we were all worn out. When we came back to the hotel, Nibbles couldn't settle down. He kept pacing around in his dressing room. He couldn't sleep with all that noise, and it was so hot. I sat by the window and held him in my hand until he went off to sleep. I almost went to sleep sitting up.

The next morning I shall *never* forget as long as I live. It involved Nibbles's most hair-raising and, I hope, the last adventure I am to record in this book.

It happened like this.

CHAPTER XV

THE CLIMAX

W E WERE all exhausted the next morning from getting to bed so late and all the excitement and noise which went on all night. I, especially, had a hectic night because every time I would doze off to sleep, I had a horrible dream that Nibbles was loose and outside my window. I would wake up in dreadful fear. Then I would turn the light on and see that he was asleep in his little room. After convincing myself that it was only a bad dream, I would go off to sleep again— only to repeat that same nightmare—and again I would get up. This happened three or four times during the night. So when morning finally came, I just couldn't get up.

Nibbles was furious with me and scolded me like anything for sleeping so late and not giving him his morning exercise, but I didn't care. I was so glad to know that he was safe in his room and not outside my window—which was eight flights up—that I just let him scold away until Mummie got me up. Then we inspected the room and closed the windows so there were no dangerous loopholes, and turned him loose for his morning playtime.

There was a door connecting with the next room, and we had several traveling bags piled up high in front of the door, and on our beds we had our overnight bags which we were packing. Nibbles was having a lovely time running in and out of our bags, up and down the curtains, and all around the room. We had to watch every move we made to keep from stepping on him. He was here one minute and there the next—hiding sunflower seeds in the waste basket, among the bedclothes—rattling around making so much noise. . . . He kept us roaring with laughter.

Then, all of a sudden, we became conscious of a dreadful silence. We listened, not a sound. Then my dream came back to me. I rushed to the windows. . . . There was no way he could get out, but I *knew* something had happened to him. I was frantic. Daddy tried to kid me out of it. He said, "I certainly feel sorry for your

"We all tried to kill him but we couldnt corner him".

children, if you ever have any. If they are out of your sight for one minute, you'll be sure something dreadful has happened to them."

I tried to relax, but I couldn't. Something told me he was in trouble. Mummie knew it too. We began looking *everywhere* for him. Daddy took the beds apart to see if there was a hole in the box springs or mattress he could have crawled into. We unpacked our overnight bags looking for him there.

Then I heard him chirp a loud chirp, just like a scream. *And it came from outside!* Eight flights up! No one else heard it, but I did. I ran to the windows, but there was no sign of him. I couldn't leave the windows—with their tiny narrow ledges. And that sickening fear that he was out there.

Daddy and Mummie were talking in low tones. By this time even Daddy was convinced that something had happened to him. But what? There wasn't any visible way of getting out of the room. We had examined every inch of it. The minutes passed. The silence grew deadlier. We were helpless, *absolutely* helpless—and we knew it. After a moment's silence Mummie said, "Let's ask God for guidance."

And with all our hearts we did. I was still talking to

God when I heard Mummie open the door into the hall. I followed her. We went down the hall. Then the corridor turned to the right and to the left. We turned left. There was a door open and a maid was running a carpet-sweeper. Mummie told her we had lost our pet chipmunk, and I asked her if she had seen him, and she said, "Oh, *that* thing—he was in here and we all tried to kill him, but we couldn't corner him, so we took the door off the fire escape and chased him out there."

I made a dash for the fire escape, but Mummie caught me and held me back, saying, "No, you stay here and keep calling him. I'll go out."

She looked up and down the fire escape, but not a sign of him. We were both praying with all our hearts. Then Mummie came in—and the next instant—*right in the place where Mummie had been standing*—there suddenly appeared *Nibbles!* He must have been clinging to the side of the stone building, and from there jumped to the fire escape and landed squarely on two of the iron railings. He is so little, he could have fallen in between them, but there he was balancing on that slippery iron railing. Eight flights up. He was shaking all over. I crept to the door, talking to him all the time, and lay down flat on my stomach on the fire escape (with

Mummie holding on to my feet), and reached out to where he was. He could hardly wait to creep into my hand. As I closed my hand gently around him, I could feel his tiny body trembling. . . . We were speechless. We just sat there on the floor with our hearts brimming over with thankfulness.

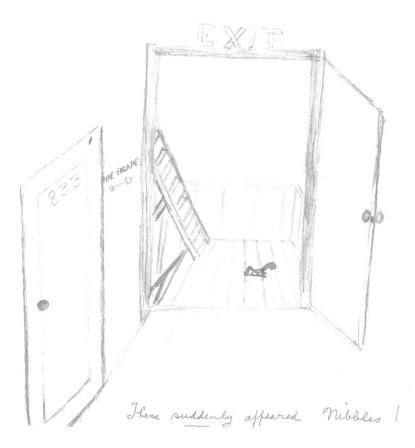

There suddenly appeared Nibbles !

CHAPTER XVI

THE END

W E LEFT Chicago that night. The studio had made reservations for us—a lovely, big drawing room on the fastest train—all the way through to California. I didn't let Nibbles out of my sight. When the porter made up our room, when we went into the diner, when the train stopped and we got off for a breath of fresh air, Nibbles was right there. People were so amazed. They had never seen a chipmunk traveling by train before. I expect he really is the world's most traveled chipmunk.

When we finally got home, Twinkle was off her head with joy. She adores Nibbles and isn't at all jealous of him. She must have sensed the time we'd had with Nibbles's adventures and how glad we were to get back home, because she just followed us around, and didn't take her eyes off Nibbles. They had a wonderful time running and playing together. It was such fun watching them.

I made some drawings of them. Twinkle posed quite nicely, but Nibbles, as usual, was all over the place . . . never still a second . . . except when there was a camera nearby. He loves to have his picture taken—but only if I am there with him. I have to be in all his photographs. He's gone like a streak if I'm not beside him.

Howard says that's because when he sees me he still thinks he's running wild. That is not meant to be a com-pliment—but somehow I think it is.

Perhaps someone will write a moving picture for Nibbles (and I'm afraid it would have to include me, too). Then you could see him in action—and see through your own eyes, instead of mine, that he is the cutest, sweetest, most adorable, *and adored* chipmunk in

THE WHOLE WORLD